D1368723

First published in Mixe-Spanish as *Ja Yäjk'o'kpë mëti'ipë ijty nëkoo tyekypye'typyënë / La Muerte pies ligeros* by Fondo de Cultura Económica, Mexico, D.F., in 2006.
First published in English-Spanish by Groundwood Books in 2007.

Groundwood Books / House of Anansi Press
110 Spadina Avenue, Suite 801, Toronto, Ontario M5V 2K4
Distributed in the USA by Publishers Group West
1700 Fourth Street, Berkeley, CA 94710

We acknowledge for their financial support of our publishing program the Government of Canada through the Book Publishing Industry Development Program (BPIDP).

Library and Archives Canada Cataloguing in Publication
Toledo, Natalia
Light foot = Pies ligeros / Natalia Toledo ; pictures by Francisco Toledo.
Text in English and Spanish. Originally published in Mixe and Spanish under title: Ja Yäjk'o'kpë mëti'ipë ijty nëkoo tyekypye'typyënë = La muerte pies ligeros.
ISBN-13: 978-0-88899-789-0
ISBN-10: 0-88899-789-2
I. Toledo, Francisco II. Title. III. Title: Pies ligeros.
PZ7.T569Li 2007   j897'.43   C2007-901142-X

Design by Óscar Reyes and Paola Álvarez
Printed and bound in China

Light Foot

Pies ligeros

Natalia Toledo
Francisco Toledo

TRANSLATED BY · TRADUCCIÓN DE
Elisa Amado

GROUNDWOOD BOOKS · LIBROS TIGRILLO
HOUSE OF ANANSI PRESS
TORONTO   BERKELEY

I wrote this story based on engravings by the artist Francisco Toledo. The engravings show Death jumping rope in Tehuantepec, where both Francisco and I were born. Tehuantepec is an isthmus – a narrow bridge of land lying between the Atlantic and Pacific oceans east of the city of Oaxaca in Mexico.

I first wrote this story in Zapotec, my native language. When I am asked which language I speak, I say "Cloud." You might wonder how anyone can speak "Cloud." Well, Zapotecs say that their language came down to them from the clouds. *Diidxa'* means language and *za* means cloud. We Zapotecs draw with words just as clouds draw different animals and other shapes in the sky.

I enjoyed writing this story very much, and I hope Zapotec, Mixtec, Mazatec, Spanish-speaking children – and children everywhere – will enjoy it, too, because every language is its own mysterious universe.

Escribí esta historia a partir de unos grabados que hizo el pintor Francisco Toledo sobre la muerte brincando el mecate con distintos animales de la región del Istmo de Tehuantepec, de donde él y yo somos.

Quise escribir este cuento en zapoteco, mi lengua natal. Cuando me preguntan qué lengua hablo, yo contesto "nube". Se preguntarán cómo se puede hablar nube, bueno, los zapotecas dicen que su lengua desciende de las nubes; *diidxa'* significa "palabra" y *za*, "nube", y así como las nubes dibujan diversas formas de animales y objetos en el cielo, los zapotecas sabemos dibujar con las palabras.

Me divertí mucho escribiendo este cuento, y espero que los niños zapotecas, chinantecos, mixes, mixtecos, mazatecos y los que hablan español también lo disfruten, pues cada lengua contiene su propio universo y su misterio.

What I am going to tell you happened a long time ago. In those days, all living beings just went on having baby after baby without stopping, but no one ever died — not people or animals.

Lo que les voy a contar sucedió hace mucho tiempo, cuando la Muerte no existía para las personas ni para los animales, cuando nadie moría sobre la Tierra y todos los seres vivos se reproducían sin parar.

Death was worried that the Earth would become too full, so she decided to clean things up a bit. She sat down under a tamarind tree and thought about what to do.

Suddenly, like a bolt of lightning, the answer came to her.

La de los pies ligeros, preocupada al ver que el mundo se sobrepoblaba, quiso limpiarlo un poco; sentada bajo un tamarindo pensó qué hacer, y como un rayo que asoma en el cielo, dijo de repente:

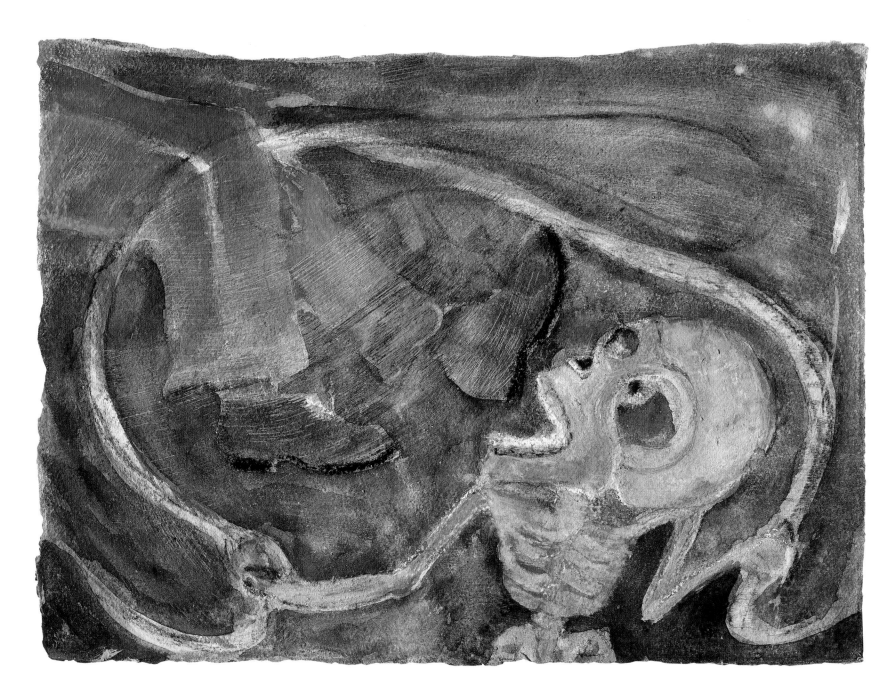

"I know. I'm going to make everyone jump rope with me. I will call all the people and all the animals. I'll dare them to keep going until they get so tired that they fall down dead from exhaustion. No one can beat me. They will all surely die, but I am immortal."

—¡Ya sé! Voy a tomar un mecate y haré que todos brinquen conmigo, llamaré al Hombre y a los animales, los retaré a saltar hasta que se cansen y mueran exhaustos. El que se dé por vencido irá muriendo. A partir de entonces nadie va a poder competir conmigo, puesto que soy eterna, y todos sin excepción tendrán que morir.

First she called Man. He was tall and
long haired, and he wore leather shoes.

Death began to skip to warm up her
rope. Then she beckoned him over to
join her.

> *I do love your shoes*
> *My dear little Man.*
> *When this winner takes all*
> *Do you have a plan?*

Al primero que llamó fue al Hombre, uno
delgado de cabello largo que llevaba
puestos unos zapatos de cuero. La Muerte
comenzó a brincar para calentar su
mecate y le hizo una seña invitándolo
a entrar.

> *Brinca y brinca el Hombrecillo*
> *burlándose de la Muerte,*
> *con pito de molinillo*
> *se quedó tieso e inerte.*

Man soon ran out of breath and died.
But Death looked longingly at his shoes.
As they say in my village, she cast a
"black-bean eye" on them. She carefully
pulled the shoes off his feet and put
them on her own, tying them up with
laces she had made from a vine.

Al Hombre se le acabó el aire y murió.
Pero la Muerte miró de reojo, como dicen
en mi pueblo, le echó "ojo de frijol" a los
zapatos que él llevaba puestos; se los quitó
con cuidado, se los puso y amarró sus
agujetas de bejuco.

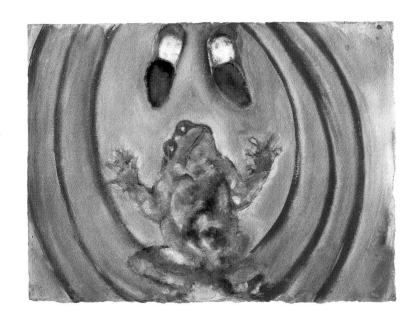

Then Death, dressed in her offbeat new
shoes, called Toad. He somersaulted
inside the rope and began to skip.

> Skip, Toad, skip.
> You know your fate.
> Wipe that smile off your lips.
> Death won't wait.

Entonces la Muerte pata dispareja llamó
al Sapo. Éste entró bajo la cuerda dando un
giro en el aire y comenzó a brincar.

> Brinca el Sapo saltarín
> con cachetes de papera,
> ya conocerás el fin
> que la muerte nunca espera...

When Toad had died, Death sang out,
"Now let the old monkey come."

Monkey rolled up his tail and ran along
the branch like a tightrope walker. Then
he leapt straight down into the game.

Jungle jumping Monkey,
Whirl your charcoal tail.
You'll be gone soon enough,
You can't possibly prevail.

Cuando el Sapo murió,
la Muerte dijo:

—¡Ahora que pase el Chango viejo!

El Chango enrolló su cola y
corrió como un equilibrista sobre la rama
donde se encontraba, después se aventó
de un salto.

Changuito de la selva oscura
mueve tu cola tiznada
aunque grites como un cura
te llevará la changada.

Not long after that, Monkey was
dead, too.

Up waddled Iguana, who had been
sunning herself on the sand. She began
to skip.

>   *Iguana, swamp dweller,*
>   *You're just digging your grave.*
>   *I'll be the winner*
>   *Though you may be brave.*

Pasado un tiempo no muy largo, murió el
Chango.

Luego vino la Iguana que se
asoleaba sobre la arena para calentar su
cuerpo frío y comenzó a brincar.

>   *Iguana del iguanar*
>   *en molito te comiera,*
>   *cavas tu tumba al brincar,*
>   *como si volver pudieras.*

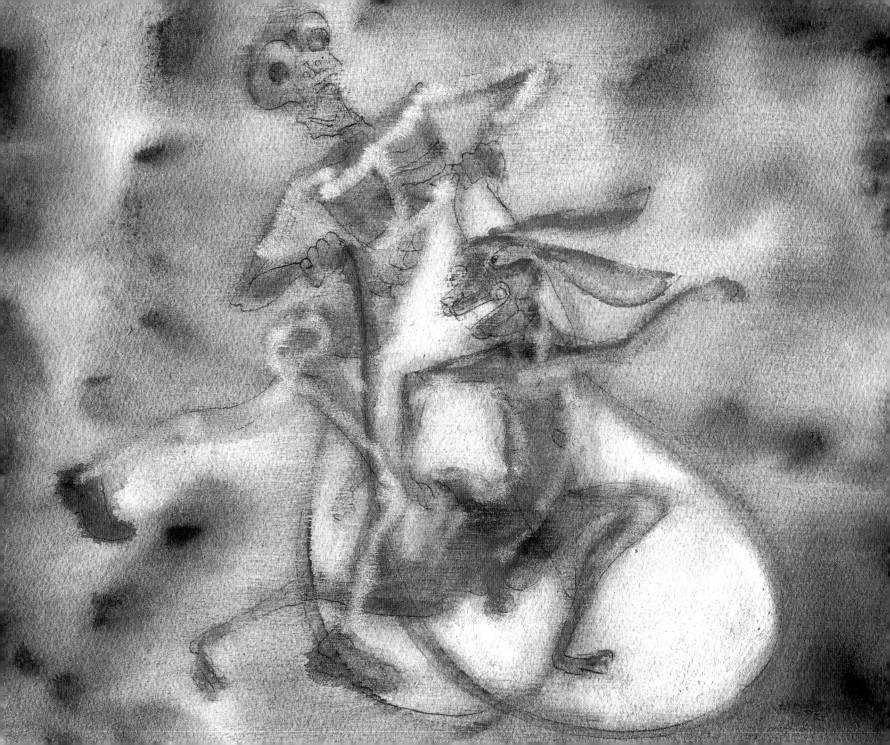

Then Death noticed Rabbit running by, with Coyote chasing after him. Death caught Coyote with her rope, and before he knew it, he was skipping and dying of laughter.

Por ahí venía corriendo el Conejo perseguido por el Coyote, pero como el Coyote es medio tonto, no vio que el Conejo se pasó de largo. La Muerte atrapó al Coyote con la cuerda y cuando el Coyote se dio cuenta ya estaba brincando, muerto de la risa.

Coyote, fast and funny,
You friendly fool.
You might as well laugh
For you'll soon be a ghoul.

And Coyote died shortly after.

Brinca, Coyote risueño,
tu risa es tu perdición,
y aunque yo no soy tu dueño
sí te llevaré al panteón.

Murió el Coyote.

Rabbit's big ears poked up from the
tall grass.

"Where is my old friend Coyote?"
he asked.

Se acababa de morir el Coyote, cuando
aparecieron las orejotas del Conejo entre la
maleza y preguntó:

—¿Dónde está mi compadre?

Death answered, "Oh, he's just here, taking a rest. He said you might as well play with me while you are waiting for him."

"All right," said Rabbit obediently, and he began to hop.

La Muerte le respondió:

—Aqui está descansando, dice que lo esperes y que brinques conmigo la reata en lo que despierta.

—Bueno —dijo el Conejo obediente y comenzó a saltar.

Rabbit, fast runner,
You've heard the old story.
I am the tortoise
So you'll soon be sorry!

And sure enough, Rabbit soon fell over
on top of his friend Coyote.

Conejo, en los cuentos ganas,
aquí pelarás los dientes
porque a mí me da la gana
ya llorarán tus dolientes.

Y el Conejo cayó muerto sobre su
compadre.

Alligator walked over slowly and
carefully. He tried to skip, but he was too
heavy. Before long he fell onto his back
and split his skin open so that he looked
like a flower opening its petals.

> *Alligator, king*
> *Of a thousand pools.*
> *You won't cheat Death,*
> *You can't change the rules.*

Entonces entró el Lagarto con su paso
delicado e intentó brincar, pero no pudo:
con el peso de su espalda se abrió como
los pétalos de una flor.

> *Lagarto de mil lagunas,*
> *novio de la flor del fango,*
> *no te vayas con ninguna,*
> *come conmigo este mango.*

And so, one by one, all the animals
jumped rope with Death. And one by one
they all died.

Así pasaron, uno por uno, todos los
animales a brincar la reata con la Muerte.

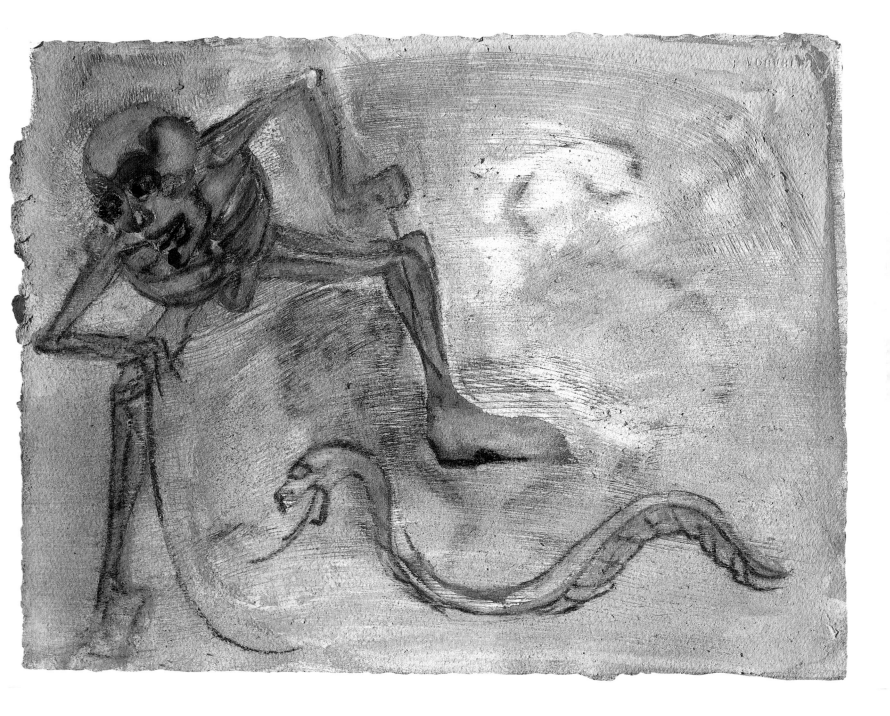

After many days had passed, Death thought that every living creature on Earth must have played her deadly game. She began to fold up her skipping rope and put it away.

That's when Grasshopper popped out of the weeds.

Y cuando ésta pensó que ya habían pasado todos, comenzó a doblar y guardar su mecate. En eso brincó del monte el Chapulín.

"Well," said Death. "How delicious. I love eating grasshopper with a tortilla, just like everyone else in Oaxaca. Come and join me."

So Grasshopper hip-hop-hopped into the game.

—Anda —dijo la Muerte—, a ti, comida de oaxaqueños, te traigo ganas.

Y el Chapulín comenzó a saltar.

Grasshopper, crooked legs
So crunchy and good.
You won't be going home
To your house in the wood.

But with a skip, jump and a leap,
Grasshopper hopped up and down, again
and again, for one day... two days...
three... four... five... six... seven... eight...
nine... ten days!

Until finally, Death paused.

Baila conmigo este son,
Chapulín bella figura;
picaré con mi aguijón
tu saltarina cintura.

Brinca que brinca el Chapulín, pasó un día,
dos, tres, cuatro, cinco, seis, siete, ocho,
nueve, ¡diez! La Muerte interrumpió y dijo:

"Who does this one think he is?" she
said. "He is making fun of me!"

So she began to whirl the rope around
like a whip — so fast that she thought no
one would be able to bear it.

But Grasshopper never seemed to grow
tired. He had cleverly hopped onto the
rope and was hanging on. Though it
looked as if he were jumping, he was
actually getting a free ride!

Death grew exhausted. Finally she
was so fed up that she threw down the
skipping rope, kicked off her shoes and
stalked off in a rage.

And from that day on, she never wore
shoes again.

—¿Qué se cree éste? ¡Se está burlando de
mí!

Entonces le hizo mole. ¿Sabes qué es
hacer mole con el mecate? Pues arreciar
con la cuerda para que los que la
brincan se cansen más rápido. Pero el
Chapulín jamás se cansó, el muy listo se
paró en el mecate y, sin hacer ningún
esfuerzo, parecía que saltaba. Cuando la
Muerte no pudo más, aventó la reata, se
quitó los zapatos, los tiró y se fue
enojada.

That's why they say that when Death comes into a house now, she is light footed, and no one can hear her.

As for Grasshopper, he had so much fun skipping with Death that he never stopped jumping.

Por eso dicen que cuando la Muerte entra en las casas no se le oye llegar, porque sus pies son ligeros y no llevan zapatos.

Al Chapulín en cambio, le quedaron tantas ganas de brincar que se quedó brincando para siempre.